For my father,
who filled me with a love of language
—D.C.O.

For Lemon and Kermit,
and all the mail carriers you barked at!
—J.C.

Visit us on the Web! rhcbooks.com

Educators and librarians, for a variety of teaching tools, visit us at RHTeachersLibrarians.com

Library of Congress Cataloging-in-Publication Data
Names: Ohanesian, Diane, author. | Chou, Joey, illustrator.
Title: If you were a garbage truck or other big-wheeled worker! / by Diane Ohanesian ; illustrated by Joey Chou.
Description: First edition. | New York : Random House Children's Books, [2022] | Audience: Ages 3–7. |
Summary: "A rhyming picture book that asks different kinds of big-wheeled workers how they feel about their various jobs"—Provided by publisher.
Identifiers: LCCN 2021009662 (print) | LCCN 2021009663 (ebook) | ISBN 978-0-593-37515-0 (hardcover) |
ISBN 978-0-593-37516-7 (library binding) | ISBN 978-0-593-37517-4 (ebook)
Subjects: LCSH: Trucks—Juvenile fiction. | Vehicles—Juvenile fiction. | Emotions—Juvenile fiction. | Stories
in rhyme. | Picture books for children. | CYAC: Stories in rhyme. | Trucks—Fiction. | Vehicles—Fiction. |
Self-acceptance—Fiction. | LCGFT: Stories in rhyme. | Picture books.
Classification: LCC PZ8.3.O355 If 2022 (print) | LCC PZ8.3.O355 (ebook) | DDC [E]—dc23

The illustrations in this book were painted digitally.

The text of this book is set in 17-point Ideal Sans.

Interior design by Nicole Gastonguay

MANUFACTURED IN CHINA
10 9 8 7 6 5 4 3 2 1
First Edition

IF YOU WERE A GARBAGE TRUCK OR OTHER BIG-WHEELED WORKER!

By Diane C. Ohanesian   Illustrations by Joey Chou

RANDOM HOUSE STUDIO ⌂ NEW YORK

Honk! Honk! Beep! Beep!
Cars and trucks race down the street.
It's another busy, big-wheeled morning.

Do they like the work they do?

Are they happy? Are they blue?

Are their honks and beeps hellos, or "Make way!" warnings?

If you were a garbage truck,

Would you cry, "Pee-yew! Yuck! Yuck!"

As smelly trash kept filling up your hopper?

Or would you feel so big and proud,
Beep your horn and shout out loud
That you're the town's most trusted waste recycler?

If you were a train,

Would you boo-choo and complain

That you have to chug along the same old track?

Or would you change your point of view
To see how many count on you
As they fill up your seats from front to back?

If you were a plow,
Would you say, "I don't know how
I make myself go out in ice and snow!"?

Or would you cheer "Hip, hip hooray!
There'll be no worries for today!
Now no one will get stuck or need a tow!"?

If you were a digger,
Would you wish that you were bigger,
Like an EXCAVATOR or a SUPER DOZER?

Or would you think, "I'm a surprise!
Even though I'm small in size,
I can dig GIGANTIC holes! I take right over!"?

If you were a crane,

Would you find it such a strain

To lift those giant loads that weigh a ton?

Or would you think, "It's up to me!
I'm as strong as I can be!
I'm the only one to get the big jobs done!"?

If you were a bus,

Would you groan and start a fuss

When kids make noise and backpacks scratch your seats?

Or would you bubble up with pride
To know you keep them safe inside
As you ride along the busy city streets?

If you were a mail truck,

Would you cry, "It's just my luck!

I spend my whole day making stops and starts!"?

Or would you know by bringing letters,
Valentines, and "please feel betters,"
You make people laugh and smile and warm their hearts?

If you were a motor home,
Would you scream, "Leave me alone!
I'm always filled with people! I need space!"?

Or would you smile and think it's neat
That passengers can sleep and eat
As you take them down the road from place to place?

If you were a fire engine,
Always standing at attention,
Would you sigh, "There's *never* time to rest!"?

Or as you spin your flashing lights,
Fighting fires day and night,
Would you remember that you always do your best?

If you were a moving van,
Would you shout, "I need a plan!
I'm sick of being packed up to the brim!"?

Or would you say, "I'll take it all!
I was made for giant hauls!
I'm a big help moving out and moving in!"?

Honk! Honk! Beep! Beep!

Cars and trucks roll down the street.

Another day is over, work is done.

Are they tired? Are they sad?

Or are they feeling awfully glad

That the work they do each day helps everyone?